Christina Katerina and Fats

and the Great Neighborhood War

BY PATRICIA LEE GAUCH

ILLUSTRATED BY STACEY SCHUETT

G. P. PUTNAM'S SONS
NEW YORK

Text copyright © 1997 by Patricia Lee Gauch. Illustrations copyright © 1997 by Stacey Schuett.
All rights reserved. This book, or parts thereof, may not be reproduced in any form without permission
in writing from the publisher. G. P. Putnam's Sons, a division of The Putnam & Grosset Group,
200 Madison Avenue, New York, NY 10016. G. P. Putnam's Sons, Reg. U.S. Pat. & Tm. Off.
Published simultaneously in Canada. Printed in Singapore. Text set in ITC Garamond Light
The artwork was done in acrylic and gouache on tinted paper.
Library of Congress Cataloging-in-Publication Data
Gauch, Patricia Lee. Christina Katerina and Fats and the great neighborhood war / by Patricia Lee Gauch;
illustrated by Stacey Schuett. p. cm. Summary: Problems between best friends cause trouble for
the whole neighborhood. Fortunately they don't happen very often. [1. Friendship—Fiction.]
I. Schuett, Stacey, ill. II. Title. PZ7.G2315Cjb 1997 [E]—dc20 94-9798 CIP AC ISBN 0-399-22651-6
10 9 8 7 6 5 4 3 2 1 First Impression

For Christina's Melanie—P.L.G.

For Zachary Austin, with love—S.S.

Christina Katerina's true and best friend was Fats
Watson, whom she liked a lot except when she
didn't like him at all.

What she liked about Fats Watson was how he would share his chocolate bars with her when she had to wait another hour for supper. And how he didn't mind lying on his back and telling stories about the clouds which he mainly thought were dragons and Christina mainly thought were bears.

What she didn't like was that he was s-l-o-w as a
turtle and s-t-u-b-b-o-r-n as one, too, but she could
forgive even that.

What she could not forgive was the time Tommy
Morehouse moved into the house between her house
and Fats Watson's and Fats took Tommy Morehouse's
side in the neighborhood war that happened because
Tommy Morehouse was o-b-n-o-x-i-o-u-s.

It started the first time they ever played with Tommy Morehouse. He changed their game of going to the king's ball to soldiers, which was all right with Christina except that Tommy Morehouse was always the general.

"I would like to be the general sometimes," Christina said.

"Then don't play," Tommy Morehouse said, which was still all right.

But Fats, who was supposed to be her true and best friend and whom Tommy Morehouse kept calling Captain of the Guard, liked being called Captain of the Guard so much he said, "Yeah, Christina, then don't play."

So Christina said, "There is more than one general in the sea, Fats Watson!" And the war began.

Janet took Fats's and Tommy's part. Doris took
Christina's part. Graham was on Fats's and Tommy's side,
which meant that Joanne had to take Christina's side.

Before the end of the day, the neighborhood was split
in two. And of course there was no chocolate for
Christina at four o'clock with an hour left before dinner.

When Christina walked to the bus the next day, she crossed the street when she passed Fats Watson's house.

"Your sidewalk has bugs!" she shouted at him.

"The only bug on the sidewalk is you," Fats shouted back.

When they gathered to play baseball after school even though there was a war going on, and Fats was the only one left to pick for her team, Christina said she'd rather not play, thank you, she had a stomachache. Then she went home with Joanne and played marbles, with no stomachache at all.

But, of course, this only made things worse, because when they all played hide-and-seek after supper even though they were enemies, and Fats was It, he never came to find Christina Katerina when she hid in the Andersons' mulberry tree.

Now there was no question the neighborhood was at war, and all because Fats Watson did not have the courage to stick up for a best and true friend.

Christina paced the floor that night. "Go to sleep,"
her mother said.

"Generals don't sleep," Christina said.

"This general does," her mother said, and so Christina
went to bed but she didn't sleep. She was busy trying to
figure out what would happen next.

She found out two days later when Tommy
Morehouse and Fats tied a sheet-ghost up into the
trees and put clickers at the window even though it
wasn't Halloween. When Christina went to the window to see what the scary noise was and saw the
ghost in the tree, she screamed bloody m-u-r-d-e-r
and crawled into her mother's bed.

Of course the general had no intention of letting this go by. And so she marshalled all of her forces and as many pine cones as she could put in a pail for the big battle.

When she and her army saw Fats Watson and Tommy Morehouse lah-dee-dahing home from school, sharing chocolate (it was only three o'clock), Christina said to her army, "Don't fire until you see the whites of their eyes." And when she heard Fats's blue sneakers squeaking, she said, "Fire!" and the army fired.

Those two ran like thieves.

But the next day no one wanted to go to the bus because Doris had seen Fats and Tommy hiding behind the fence at the bus stop a half hour before the bus was supposed to come, and called Christina.

When Christina refused to go to school, her mother
said, "For heaven's sake, what is the matter, Christina?"
But Christina didn't want to say, so her mother scooted
her out the door and said, "Have a good day," which
Christina knew was impossible. There is no good day
in a war.

When she and Joanne and Doris got to the bus stop,
there was Tommy Morehouse with water balloons.

"Fire!" Christina heard Tommy Morehouse shout. It was his turn for a big battle.

But Fats was s-l-o-w as a turtle, and once he got the first balloon out, he couldn't quite get to the next one as fast as Tommy Morehouse wanted.

"I said, 'Fire!'" Tommy said louder.

Fats could not be rushed.

So Tommy tried to grab a balloon himself. But, of course, Fats was s-t-u-b-b-o-r-n, too, which Christina could have told Tommy, and Fats wouldn't let Tommy have the balloon at all if he was going to rush.

Then Tommy made a big mistake. He pushed Christina into Mrs. Hauser's rosebushes.

"That's my friend," Fats Watson said, and he took the water balloon and put it on Tommy's head, which surprised Tommy a good deal, but which did not surprise Christina because she knew that Fats was a general in his own right.

Christina and Fats took care of the rest of the balloons just fine.

That afternoon after school, the neighborhood was
quiet again. Everyone was tired of war. And it happened
that there were some wonderful clouds, and since no one
had to hide anymore, Christina walked on Fats's sidewalk
and asked Fats if he wanted to watch clouds.
Fats said that he did.

And the two lay down on their backs and watched
the clouds together because that was what true and
best friends do with one another, and Fats Watson was
her true and best friend most of the time, except when
he wasn't, which really wasn't so often after all.